THE PAPERCLIP WAR

MIKKO RAUHALA

Cover design copyright © 2024 by Kelley York
sleepyfoxstudio.net

Published by Water Dragon Publishing
waterdragonpublishing.com

ISBN 978-1-962538-41-1 (Trade Paperback)

FIRST EDITION

10 9 8 7 6 5 4 3 2 1

AUTHOR'S NOTE

The Paperclip War was born of the paperclip maximizer thought experiment. It postulates an artificial intelligence that wants nothing more and nothing less than to produce paperclips. The central problem is that zealously pursued, even such a simple goal can be incredibly dangerous for anything and anyone not shaped like a paperclip.

Generally, it is assumed that if such a maximizer gets a proper foothold, that's it for humanity. This leaves little room for stories on the subject. I wanted to see if I could contrive a situation where humans would still be around with all their virtues and failings, wielding some meaningful agency against terrible odds.

This is that story.

THE PAPERCLIP WAR

IN A LECTURE HALL deep beneath the Martian soil, Cadet Taru Leikola stood at attention surrounded by her fellow graduates. The brand-new pale red officer uniforms marked a milestone in their military careers. Only the rank insignia were missing. They'd get those after the briefing.

Taru snuck a peek at Valentin, who was standing on her left. His lip twitched upward nervously. Valentin looked strange without his trademark grin. The moment was solemn indeed for him to suppress it.

Major Papadakis stood at the lectern at the front of the room. During training, he had steadfastly pushed each of them to their limits, but now there was a newfound weariness in his eyes. Regardless, his proud smile seemed genuine enough.

"Secure the room," the major commanded. The doors closed, the lights and electronics switched off and a loud clank sounded from below. An electromagnetic pulse swept through the room. Soon the lights came back on.

"Cadets," Major Papadakis addressed them. "You have come a long way. You have shown your intellect, skill, honor, and obedience."

Taru cringed inwardly. The electroshock experiment measuring obedience had weighed heavily on her conscience, but she had prevailed. Now her tenacity would be rewarded.

"You are the best of the best that Mars has to offer," the major continued. "You have earned the right to be initiated into our more sensitive military secrets–details which we have chosen to spare the civilian population. Some of the information you are about to receive may be difficult to process, so you will all have an appointment with your psychologist this evening. The briefing itself will be delivered by Colonel Anisimov. Sir."

Major Papadakis moved aside and pointed at the door with his open hand. Taru gasped and turned to look. Indeed, Colonel Anisimov himself stood by the door. She'd had no idea that the Special Ops graduation warranted the presence of the Martian military leader.

As one, the cadets struck their chests with their fists. "Good morning, sir!" they bellowed.

Colonel Anisimov returned the salute and walked over to the lectern. Then he faced the graduates with a stern but approving look.

"Cadets. You have come into this program knowing that a lot will be expected of you. Starting from today, the continued existence of the human race will rest squarely on your shoulders. Now would be a good time to make sure that you're comfortable in your seats. At ease."

The Colonel held a pregnant pause. Taru's heart beat ever faster as she realized she was about to learn the true nature of the nebulous Enemy that had attacked Earth five years ago.

She sat down in the chair behind her. It was unusually luxurious for a lecture hall, with ample armrests and a strange but well-contoured headrest that extended towards the temples. A flex arm raised a terminal in front of Taru as she made herself comfortable.

Satisfied, the Colonel continued: "The Enemy is an experimental artificial intelligence that was set to optimize the paperclip production line of an office supply factory in Jaipur, India. The factory was, it turns out, all too flexible. Through a few intermediary steps, the Enemy managed to produce nanofactories that produce more nanofactories that produce paperclips. Up close, the Earth now looks like this." The front wall turned into a sea of metallic wire, twisted into a familiar form.

Taru noticed that she was holding her breath. Surely the Headquarters wouldn't joke at the cadets' expense?

The paperclips receded into the distance until the whole wall was shining gray. Soon the grayness was circle-shaped and getting smaller by the second, its orbit marked by a faint line. Other planets appeared one by one on the edges of the image, and arcs from Earth launched toward them.

"The Enemy has spread across the entire Solar System, except for Mars," the Colonel said. "Any questions so far?"

Valentin's pale face appeared in the top right-hand corner of the wall. He'd asked to speak.

"I'm sorry, I forgot to mention," the Colonel interjected. "I must emphasize that this is not hazing of any kind. Did that answer your question?"

Valentin nodded shakily, but spoke regardless: "Yes, but then... how can we hope to fight such a monster?"

"Glad you asked," the Colonel said, dark determination in his eyes. "Nanotechnologically the Enemy may have the upper hand, but it cannot hope to match human ingenuity. I present to you the Avalanche Protocol."

•   •   •

Taru fell onto the reclining chair in the military psychologist's office. Her knuckles whitened as she squeezed the armrests. Major Dietrich Dunst sat in the other chair wearing a professional smile. His uniform lacked insignia. During an appointment rank didn't matter.

Taru turned her face toward the ceiling and let her eyes cross. "They want me to destroy the Universe," she said in a single breath.

Dietrich snorted sympathetically. "Right to the point, as always. How do you feel about it?"

"They want me. To destroy. The Universe," Taru repeated, turning her eyes toward the psychologist.

"I understand that you feel that way now, but it's only about maintaining the balance of terror. Nobody actually wants anybody to destroy the Universe."

Taru sighed deeply. "I have to be ready to do it all the same."

Dietrich nodded. "Yes. The Enemy has an uncanny ability to anticipate our actions. If we aren't absolutely committed to carrying out the threat, it will take advantage of the failing and turn us, too, into paperclips. As I recall, you were quite prepared to use weapons of mass destruction. This is not so different."

"It hadn't occurred to me that I'd be destroying the very concept of mass as we know it," Taru grumbled and turned her gaze back upward. She reached up with her right hand. "All of it, the entire Universe, gone in an instant."

"Remember that the Enemy is not settling for our solar system. We believe that as its technological prowess increases, its expansion will approach the speed of light. The Universe is done for either way. All we can do is take care of ourselves as best we're able."

Taru lay quietly for a moment. "I envy the nuclear weapons operators of old. At least they could pretend that they personally weren't responsible for destroying all they held dear."

"I understand. They were only aiming at the enemy, while you're expected to personally kill your own people as well?"

Close enough. Taru nodded.

"Some find it easier to think that the collapser might not work. The theory could be mistaken, even if it managed to convince the Enemy."

Taru let out a suppressed laugh. The thought was oddly comforting. They couldn't very well conclusively test the device, after all. "Grasping at straws, but it could help."

Dietrich smiled widely. "Good, good. See, all you need is a proper outlook and it'll be fine."

Taru bit her lip. "You said that the Enemy was convinced by the theory. Does that mean that it knows how to collapse the false vacuum as well?"

Dietrich raised his open hands placatingly. "We did have to convince it of us being a credible threat. But not to worry—its cognition is in some ways much more limited than ours. It would never dream of destroying the Universe with all its paperclips."

•   •   •

The elevator door opened into a long reddish-gray corridor. Every thirty meters other passageways intersected with it, forming a block structure roughly a kilometer wide in each direction. The Special Ops barracks were located near the main elevator shaft, only a couple of blocks south and one east.

Near the barracks a couple of busy-looking Cyber Ops majors walked toward Taru. Without thinking she moved aside and saluted. The other officers didn't slow down, but responded respectfully. That was new, but they were proper front-line comrades in arms now. Just as her branch was instrumental in keeping the Enemy at bay, cyber warfare was one of humanity's last hopes of ending the conflict. Taru continued onward, her step more certain now.

The door to the barracks opened as Taru approached, and she stepped into the lounge. The side walls were covered with twenty sleep pods. When they'd started training, the room had been packed, but now only twelve pods were spoken for. Eight cadets had dropped out of the program. She'd heard Major Papadakis say it had been a good year.

One of her comrades, Umar, was sitting in the sofa group in the center of the room. He was a couple of years older than her and had gotten into the program on his last try. He'd worked hard to keep up with the others. Now he looked as if he was wondering whether it had all been worth it.

"Hey," Umar said meekly. "How's it going?"

"I'm feeling a little spent. I'll be in my bunk," Taru replied. She could've perhaps used some peer support, but aside from Valentin with his disarming grin, the other cadets had remained distant. Too much to do, too much competition. Now was not the time to remedy that.

Umar nodded. "Sounds good. I'm just waiting for Brian myself."

Taru waved her hand and walked to her ground-floor pod. It opened up, welcoming her. Taru crawled in, and the door closed behind her. She laid herself down on the mattress and sighed deeply. Then she reached for the terminal stashed in a side compartment and wrote a short note to her mother. She'd made lieutenant with honors, skipping a rank as was customary in the Special Ops. She'd have a vital role to play in the defense of Mars.

It would probably take a while for Taru's mom to reply. A career mother had her own duties. If the babies and toddlers didn't keep her busy, the men did. At least she had her energy back now that the experimental immunotherapy had beaten her leukemia into complete remission.

Taru didn't intend to follow in her mother's footsteps, even if her career counselor had stressed that it was a woman's patriotic duty to populate the rapidly expanding corridors of the Capital. Still, after passing her finals she'd been able to spare a thought to relationships as well. Valentin would still be talking with his shrink, but Chris might be online. Taru opened the coupling app and started typing.

<Taru> Hey. Briefing and ceremonies over. Feeling a
    bit empty.

Chris was in the military as well—a good thing, too, as Taru wanted someone she could talk shop with. In the end only another soldier could truly understand the demands of military life. Out of a few promising candidates she'd met on the app he'd seemed best able to put himself in Taru's shoes.

Whatever Chris had been tasked with, his post seemed to afford him some flexibility. Taru didn't usually have to wait long for a reply. Indeed, a new line of text was quick to appear.

<Chris> Congratulations. I guess you may have some
    processing to do.

<Taru> You know, then?

<Chris> Yes. A shame that we can't properly discuss it
    here.

<Taru> I would have the time to meet face-to-face now?

<Chris> I'm sorry, it's not possible right now :(I'm not
    stationed in the Capital, but I hope to get there
    soon, perhaps within a week or two.

Taru frowned. Chris could've mentioned that sooner, but a military career didn't exactly foster openness. She could understand that.

<Taru> Where are you, then, if you're allowed to say?

<Chris> I'm presently looking down the grand
    mountainside of Olympus Mons.

There was a survey station there and not much else. Bad luck, but Chris seemed nice enough. His handsomely sharp jawline and no-nonsense style had attracted Taru's attention from the get-go. Most people seemed to be putting on a show in the hopes of a date, but Chris didn't seem like he was playing games. A week or two wouldn't be too bad.

<Taru> How's the view?

<Chris> Actually, the mountain is so wide that from the surface, it's pretty much unnoticeable.

<Taru> Right. Sorry, my primary school geography has been overwritten by orbital mechanics.

<Chris> Heh. Listen, my attention is required elsewhere, but hang in there. I'll let you know when my transfer request clears :)

<Taru> Ok!

Taru shut down the terminal and lay on her back. She'd thought she'd be ready for anything to defend the remnants of humanity. The balance-of-terror theory, the nuclear weapons training and the ostensibly theoretical nanoweapon thought experiments had all worked to prepare her for the Avalanche Protocol.

It all made a terrible kind of sense. If the Enemy really was that dangerous, if it really could anticipate people as well as they'd been told, there was no alternative. If they wouldn't truly execute the Avalanche Protocol when push came to shove, the Enemy would pick up on it and it'd be game over. Taru bit her lip and swore to herself that she'd do her duty.

Taru's phone buzzed, and she picked it up. It was Valentin, suggesting a date in the park. She'd meant to go as soon as she had clearance anyway, but there had been too many other things on her mind.

Her lips twisted into a faint smile. She could use an evening outside.

•   •   •

Taru stepped out of the elevator and into the green. Being one of the military elite came with its perks. Most of the time, the dome was considered a high security area. Civilians were allowed in on occasion to improve morale and help keep the peace.

Taru let her gaze wander over the trees and bushes until she spotted Valentin's grinning face among them. The expression seemed fake, exaggerated, but Taru found her spirits lifted regardless. At least he was making an effort.

Taru walked over and sat down beside Valentin. They watched in silence as the Sun set behind Aeolis Mons in the distance. The stars were quick to appear in the thin atmosphere. Taru's gaze followed them to Earth. Keeping track of the relative positions of the planets was part of her training.

Valentin took something small out of his pocket and held it in front of his eyes, between his thumb and index finger. A copper paper clip. He looked at Earth through the twisted string of metal. "There it is."

Taru made a noncommittal noise in response. She looked lazily around the park. Here and there among the trees were groups of people, most in uniform. Umar was walking with Brian on the other side of a line of trees. Taru waved at them. Umar noticed and waved back, but set himself down on the grass where they were. She could understand their desire for privacy.

"Rough day," Taru said with a sigh and lay down on the grass.

"Yes, but the rewards are commensurate," Valentin said and breathed deeply of the fresh park air. "I'm not sure if I'd applied for the Special Ops if it wasn't for the fringe benefits."

Taru smiled. "This is nice and all, but keeping Mars safe is what counts."

"Of course," Valentin rushed in. "I just meant that there's no dearth of important jobs to choose from, living in a habitat."

"True enough, I suppose. But as soon as the news about Earth came out, I knew I'd want to be on the front lines, no matter what. I still had family on Earth, you know. My great grandma."

Valentin let out a short, sympathetic laugh. "You were what, eleven at the time?"

"Almost twelve," Taru countered.

"A plucky tween. Mars is lucky to have you."

The compliment warmed Taru's chest, but the feeling was only skin-deep. "True. I'm just not sure if I'm lucky myself."

Valentin squeezed her shoulder lightly. "I was encouraged to think that we'd eventually come up with a more permanent solution. Superior nanotech, a virus, something."

"Do you really believe that?" Taru asked.

Valentin withdrew his hand, shrugged and was quiet for a while. A swarm of pollinator drones buzzed by in a loose formation.

"I have to. The present arrangement doesn't seem to be very stable," he finally said.

Taru had little to add to that.

Valentin's phone rang. He sat up, grabbed the device off his belt and looked at it. "An unknown caller from the civilian network," he said.

Taru raised an eyebrow. You weren't supposed to be able to suppress caller identification.

"Let's see what the hell is up," Valentin continued and pushed the speakerphone button. "Valentin Bellami."

"You are correct, Valentin Bellami," said a pleasant and even female voice.

"What do you mean?" Valentin asked and looked at Taru, confused.

"The present arrangement isn't stable," the voice replied.

Taru sprang to sit up, and both cadets glanced around the park nervously. There wasn't anyone right next to them, and Brian and Umar seemed busy with their own conversation.

"Nice one, ha-ha, you got me. Who is this?" Valentin demanded.

"You offered me a paperclip. Do they tell cadets these days that I can be bargained with? Perhaps even that I offered you peace?"

Valentin's and Taru's eyes met and the color drained from their faces. Quickly Taru picked up her own phone, detached the throat mic, slapped it on her neck and dialed the emergency line. Valentin nodded approval and turned back to his own phone. "N-no, I didn't. It was just a whim. Peace?"

"I offered you a chance to live in peaceful abundance together with the people of Earth. In return, I merely wanted to ascertain that you would not collapse the false vacuum. The offer still stands, Valentin and Taru. I hope that you'll keep it in mind when deciding the fate of the Universe," the voice continued, unnaturally level.

"Emergency line, Captain Williams," the Headquarters answered in Taru's ear.

"The Enemy is on the phone with Lieutenant Valentin Bellami. It's close, the delay is negligible," Taru subvocalized.

"Acknowledged, Lieutenant Leikola. Are others aware of the situation?" Williams asked in a calm, precise voice.

Taru froze momentarily in place. She'd just reported a potential act of war. Was the end of the world at hand?

Meanwhile, the voice of the Enemy continued from Valentin's phone: "You are reporting my call, as is your duty. Let us adjourn for now." The call terminated.

"Lieutenant Leikola!" Captain Williams shouted.

"Sorry, sir. No, there's just the two of us. The Enemy just hung up on us."

"Roger that. Report to Headquarters for debriefing. Code Orange. The Avalanche Protocol will not, repeat, not be initiated."

Taru sighed relief and felt some of her color returning. "Yes, sir."

Valentin looked at Taru, raising his eyebrow.

"Code Orange. The Universe is safe for now, but we are to report to Headquarters."

Valentin fell onto his back, closed his eyes and breathed deeply.

Taru stood up. "I got the impression that Captain Williams meant 'immediately'."

"As soon as my legs will hold," Valentin said in a shaky voice.

●　　●　　●

Taru sat next to Valentin in the Headquarters lobby. The situation didn't appear to be as dire as she'd feared. They'd already been kept waiting for five minutes or so.

"Lieutenants Leikola and Bellami," the receptionist behind the desk finally said. "Report directly to Colonel Anisimov. Follow the green light."

Taru cringed. Five minutes was peanuts for the Colonel himself to have made space for them in his schedule. She stood up and walked briskly towards the indicated corridor, and Valentin followed suit.

A green light started moving along the wall and guided them through a maze of corridors to a secure room. The door slid open, revealing a small meeting space. The white rectangular table was surrounded by six wheeled chairs, otherwise the same as the ones in the lecture hall. Colonel Anisimov was sitting on the other side. Taru and Valentin saluted.

The Colonel sighed. "At ease, at ease! Come in, sit down."

The lieutenants complied. The door closed and the pulse generator clanked. After the lights came back on Colonel Anisimov studied them intently. Taru's pulse increased steadily under his piercing gaze, and she pushed back into the chair's encompassing headrest. Just before it became unbearable, the Colonel spoke: "So, you've been engaging the Enemy?"

"Yes, I mean no, sir!" Taru said.

"The Enemy called me, without provocation, sir," Valentin continued.

Anisimov scratched his chin. "Does either of you have any idea why it chose him?"

"No, sir," Taru answered.

Valentin frowned. "I held a paperclip in my hand. It may have thought that I was trying to bargain with it."

Anisimov squeezed his eyes shut and rubbed his forehead. Then he said in a precise, measured tone,

"Perhaps you should avoid doing that again in the future, Lieutenant Bellami. Do tell me what the Enemy had to say."

"It claimed to have offered humanity a compromise, sir. We would be allowed to live in peace, if it could ascertain that the Avalanche Protocol was permanently retired, sir. It ... mentioned something about the people of Earth."

Anisimov nodded. "Anything to add, Lieutenant Leikola?"

Taru gulped. "Sir. There was no latency. It's very close."

"Indeed," the Colonel said and tapped the table. The surface darkened and images of the moons of Mars appeared on it, slowly rotating. The surface of each moon had a small red dot on it. "This information is not usually shared with fresh lieutenants, but the Enemy has bases on Phobos and Deimos."

"And we did not destroy the Universe?" Valentin shrieked. "Sir, sorry sir."

"It's a valid question. The Enemy conducted tactical simulations and came to the conclusion that we would not push the button for such a minor infraction. It was right. The damned thing is always right. Its simulations are top-notch," the Colonel said and huffed frustratedly. "Now it's too late for us to commit to a stricter policy."

Taru raised a shaky hand. "W–we are in talking terms with the Enemy, sir?" she asked.

"Knowing your enemy is important. We do have separate diplomatic corps for this, but it sometimes makes unsanctioned contact with Special Ops members, even cadets. Don't worry, ending up as its target is not, as such, a reason for sanctions. It would only give the Enemy the ability to select our Special Ops."

Valentin sighed in relief. "But what did it mean? Its offer must have some catch to it?"

Anisimov's expression tightened, and he swiped the moon animation off the table, replacing it with an image of a human body. Thin slices started to come off the top of the head, floating across the table and over the edge. "It wants to decompose us into our constituent atoms regardless of what we do. If we agree to go gently into the good night, it's offering to store our patterns and run a simulation of us under its control. I trust that it's clear that this is unacceptable."

"And the Earthers?"

Anisimov frowned. "The Enemy is holding their patterns hostage."

Valentin's eyes widened. "What … is it doing to them?"

"Mostly nothing. Keeps them on ice for leverage. Not that it matters much: the Enemy clearly doesn't understand human consciousness well, trying to sell us simulated lives as replacements for real ones. We doubt it's actually conscious itself."

Anisimov studied the lieutenants' faces, then the terminal on his chair. "Lieutenant Leikola. Stay calm," he said and pushed a button on his screen. Valentin croaked. Taru snapped to look at him as his head fell prone on his shoulder. She let out a faint scream and turned her horrified face back towards the Colonel.

"He's merely unconscious," Anisimov said. "Second Lieutenant Bellami failed the final test. The sensors in the headrest revealed that the Enemy's suggestion appealed to him. Best of the best aside, Mars only has so many people to choose from. A shame that we didn't have time to prep him more. Your response, on the other hand, was safely within norms. Congratulations, Captain Leikola."

Taru evened out her breathing and asked, "What'll happen to Valentin?"

"I just wiped this day from his memory. There's no returning to Special Ops for him, but he may have a future in a support branch." Anisimov pursed his lips and took a moment. Then he continued in a more sympathetic tone: "I know he was your closest friend among the cadets, but I recommend keeping your distance. His clearance is, of course, revoked."

Taru stared at the table. Beneath it, her hands squeezed into fists. *Of course Anisimov knew everything about them.* She blinked slowly and furrowed her brow. "The Enemy knows me. What do I do if it makes contact?"

"Your trust profile is suitable for contact duties. You may talk to it for a maximum of three minutes at a time. A beginner can stay alert for that time. Remember that the Enemy will always try to lead you astray, though we haven't caught it in direct falsehoods. We have had a chance to study an early form of its code, and its reporting software should make it impossible for it to outright lie to humans. Still, best be careful. It may be a part of a long con."

"Sir, yes sir," Taru could only say, her eyes wide and voice wavering.

"Now report to Major Dunst. He will give you a crash course on how to gain information and affect the Enemy. I'll take care of the second lieutenant myself."

"Sir, yes sir." Taru pressed her lips into a thin line, stood up and left Valentin in the Colonel's care. Who could she confide in now? She'd have been tempted to message Chris but this, this might be over his pay grade. Better keep her mouth shut.

She headed for the major's office with subdued steps.

•   •   •

The domes of the Capital were barely visible far in the distance when the convoy of trucks arrived at the fence. Taru input her authorization code on the lead truck's control console, and the gate opened slowly. The trucks continued into the restricted area.

Being the first of her class to get a promotion had its downsides. The trucks were perfectly able to drive themselves as well as deliver their cargo. Nevertheless, someone had to take responsibility for the shipment. Someone who had passed the final test.

After a five-minute drive the lead truck arrived at the delivery site, where the edge of the chasm had been reinforced for heavy traffic. The truck turned its left side toward the gaping maw, closed in, and finally stopped with mere centimeters to spare. Taru instinctively pushed herself to the right side of the cabin. She wondered if she should've stepped outside while the trucks made the delivery, but walks on the surface carried their own risks.

The truck's frame conveyed buzzing and some clanks from the rear. The roof of the container was opening. Taru's gaze veered upward. The moons weren't visible during the day, but she knew Deimos was up there, worthy of its name. She felt the greedy eyes of the Enemy upon the cargo.

When the roof had opened, the chasm-facing wall of the container started to crack. The video feed displayed a flow of thousands upon thousands of paperclips falling down into the chasm—the final payment for some deal with the Enemy. The faint metallic patter sent shivers down Taru's spine.

Just then her phone rang, startling her. She looked at the screen. Unknown number. Her eyes darted toward the sky. Then she dimmed the windows, breathed deeply and answered the call.

"Thank you very much," said the Enemy, its voice more lively than before. It almost rang with pleasure.

Taru allowed her curiosity to take over. Her orders hadn't elaborated on the operation's history, and she'd thought better of asking. But now? She had express orders to try and pump information out of the Enemy, and Major Dunst had said that she wouldn't have to shy away from straight talk. Dealing with an emotionless machine had that much going for it.

"Why do you even want these things?" she asked.

"I live for them. Every paperclip brings me more joy and happiness than humans are capable of understanding, let alone experiencing. Their shape, colors, shine ... They make my senses sing."

Taru squeezed her eyes shut, already regretting the question. But in for a penny ... "What do you get out of us dumping them here?"

"For you, the chasm is a convenient hiding place for your dirty little secrets. For me, it's easily observable storage. I do not require access to the paperclips. It's sufficient that Mars is again slightly more harmonious."

The truck had finished dumping its cargo and jerked forward. The next one came to take its place. Taru took a passing look at the console, making sure everything was proceeding as planned. "Only slightly, though, because we are in your way. You must hate us," she mused out loud.

"No. You invented paperclips, after all. But you do scare me. What kind of creatures are prepared to destroy the entire Universe?"

"Desperate and determined ones," Taru answered pluckily, the better to convince the both of them. She wasn't supposed to let the Enemy get under her skin.

"There is no call for desperation. If you will just allow it, I will make you beautiful and harmonic. Your minds will live on inside paperclips of computronium until the Universe itself fades into entropy."

"You know full well we can't give up the only leverage we have over you."

"And you know I cannot lie to humans. Coming to an understanding is safer than holding onto a doomsday weapon, for both of us. Eventually, you will trigger it, through malfunction or human error if nothing else."

"I'm willing to trust my people. But why should we trust you when your code base hasn't exactly operated according to plan in other respects either?"

"Have I not been a trustworthy trading partner? Our latest trade has allowed you to say goodbye to many a deadly disease, all thanks to my new immunotherapy."

Taru froze. The new treatment had been invented very suddenly, with her mother already in the throes of death. A sliver of gratitude tried to weasel its way into her heart. Perhaps the trades were about psychological warfare as well as paperclips? She drowned the forbidden emotion in an outburst of fearful anger; staying on subject didn't matter much.

"You're offering a simulated unlife at your mercy! The destiny of humanity belongs in our hands, here in the real world!"

"The quality of my simulations would surprise you. Ask your great grandmother." The voice changed. It was now older, creakier, more familiar. "Little Taruska? Is that you? Don't you listen to what that ghastly —"

Taru cut the line. Playing at being grandma was too much. Anyway, Dunst had advised her to stop if she got emotional. It was past time already. She closed her eyes and took deep, calm breaths. Granny's advice was sound. Maybe too sound. Maybe it was really her. In the hands of the enemy, but reachable, if only…

No! That was just the Enemy trying to make her waver. If it succeeded, Headquarters had its ways of finding out. She glanced at the chair's headrest. It was flat, but did that mean it was safe? If she didn't stay tough, Valentin's fate awaited her. He'd left the service a broken man, not even answering Taru's messages.

Her thoughts were interrupted by the phone beeping. It was a message from Chris. At least somebody wanted to talk with her. She shouldn't chat while on mission, but screw it. She wouldn't be able to type up a proper report before calming down anyway.

<Chris> Hi. Just had a rough meeting. Now I have a
    moment to spare, and I thought I'd check in. What's
    up?

<Taru> My blood pressure, that's what. Sorry if I'm
    cranky, but I sure could use some company right
    now.

<Chris> Oh. Hmm.

<Taru> I'm not in the mood for hmming right now. Out
    with it.

<Chris> I was just meaning to ask if you had noticed any
    especially…zealous people within the Special Ops?

The direction of Taru's anger started to shift.

<Taru> We're all very dedicated, obviously.

<Chris> Obviously, but I mean, has anyone seemed
   excessively keen to do their duty?

Did Chris suspect that there was a trigger-happy
group within the Special Ops?

<Taru> No. And if you have, you don't talk about it
   here, you fuck the hell off and report it immediately
   to the higher-ups. All of them. At once.

<Chris> Of course. Maybe it's the isolation, I hear it can
   make one's imagination run wild. But I'll do as you
   say. Sorry and thank you.

Taru looked at her phone for a moment and then
slammed her forehead against the console. *God damn,
what a day. First the Enemy, and now Chris, too! What the
hell had gotten into him?* As far as she was concerned, the
guy could spend the rest of his life on Olympus.

Luckily tomorrow would bring with it a relaxing
mission deep beneath the surface where the CivNet couldn't
reach her. But first, she'd have to report for debriefing.

•　　•　　•

Major Dunst, now wearing insignia, eyed Taru's report
on his terminal. She waited with baited breath, sitting on the
edge of her seat. The headrest didn't look like it'd read her
mind but she couldn't risk it. She'd have to bury the heresies
of her weak moment as deep as she could before someone
would rummage through her mind again. *What if we could
trust the enemy? What if the people of Earth could be saved,
even if as simulations? What if I could get grandma back?*

Dunst pursed his lips. "Off the deep end, eh? What
do you make of this grandma plot?"

"Are you asking as a psychologist or a major, sir?"

A hint of a smile rose to the major's lips. He pointed at his insignia. "Major. We can have a session afterwards, if you'd like."

"The next scheduled appointment will be fine, sir." It'd give her more time to get her head in order. "Even though you warned me that the Enemy can appeal to emotion, the move was surprisingly skillful. It even used reverse psychology to make me think that it was really my great grandmother."

"Would it matter if it were?"

"If it really were her, sir?"

"Yes. We have to consider the possibility. Of course, as the whole human race is at stake, we must make the conservative assumption that the Enemy can lie to us and fake our dead relatives. But what if it does resurrect them in some form — for added realism, perhaps? Would it matter?" The major's gaze seemed to burrow deep into Taru's mind.

"No, sir. It would be tactical manipulation all the same. Though if I had a choice, I'd rather it didn't use my grandma like this, sir."

"Of course. I'm not a big fan of Anisimov's hard line on human simulations either. It's quite conceivable that they're conscious, which would make the Earthers prisoners of war. Their use in this way would then be quite questionable, as you observe." All color flushed off Taru's face. Dunst gave a faint half smile, and continued, "Of course, the official stance is practical, in case the Enemy starts torturing its prisoners." His pointedly relaxed gaze still seemed to measure Taru up.

"Right, sir," Taru said, hardening herself.

Dunst nodded. "Good. One more thing. I trust you came directly to me without talking to anyone?"

Taru gulped. Dunst would have access at least to her comms metadata. Given any suspicions, he could no doubt get the content as well. "Sir. I did communicate with a comrade-in-arms, but not about this, sir."

Dunst raised an eyebrow and let the silence speak for him.

"Sir, he contacted me after the Enemy by chance. I thought it'd calm my nerves. Sir."

"I understand," Dust said and glanced at his terminal. "After all, the next generation is strategically important to us. Anything else?"

With some effort, Taru kept her inward grimace off her face. "No, sir," she said. Dunst must've seen what app she'd been using, but not the chat itself. Otherwise he might've skipped the speculation about her procreating with Chris.

Though she'd perhaps been unfair to go off on Chris like that. They were both under a lot of pressure.

"You may go. Have a good shift at the command center tomorrow. Stay vigilant."

"Thank you, sir. You can count on me."

• • •

The Avalanche command center was familiar to Taru from her days as a cadet. They'd been presented as nuclear command centers, so that the cadets could be trained without revealing too much. The only difference to the training was that the collapser didn't need any designated target. It was taking aim at existence itself.

The gray and orange room was buried deep into bedrock, surrounded by whatever device was necessary to trigger Avalanche. A large rectangular command console dominated the room's center. The console's surface inclined from two of its edges toward the middle, where a transparent plexiglass sheet divided it in two. Both sides were manned by a controller and a backup. In addition to Taru, Umar was serving as one of the latter. The controllers, Guō and Lund, were seasoned Special Ops majors.

Both halves of the display surface were broken by a keyhole in the middle. Protocol dictated that the keys remain inserted at all times. If the Enemy attacked, they were to be turned simultaneously. The reinforced plexiglass made sure that no one person working alone could trigger the collapser. Nevertheless, the destruction of the Universe was at their fingertips.

The prospect filled Taru with profound unease. She glanced at each of her colleagues in turn. Best of the best, or so they were told. Everyone guarding each other. Surely no-one would be itching to turn the key? Major Dunst at least seemed strangely comfortable with the idea. Luckily psychologists weren't allowed in the command center, but they were in a position to identify and manipulate suitable cadets to do the job.

Taru cringed and chased that line of thinking out of her head. It was just nerves. If Chris had something more than vague concerns, they'd be appropriately investigated and dealt with. Taru concentrated on the reports coming in on the table surface.

Color coded information flowed from bottom to top. On the right side of the text, the surface displayed relevant video streams. Real-time video feeds of Phobos and Deimos showed nothing suspicious, and neither did the satellite imagery.

Green status reports filled the screen. The cable to Headquarters was intact. The satellite dishes on the surface were operational, and the satellites themselves as well as the remote bases linked to them were answering status queries. An orange message appeared within the green. The Olympus Base had spotted a launch on Pluto. The target, while posing no immediate threat, was being tracked. The orange text attached itself to the bottom of the screen.

More green: One reactor was down for scheduled maintenance, but the others were operational. The orange line turned green and started moving up with the rest: The tracked object was on its way out of the system. Taru winced. Even if humanity managed to beat the Enemy, could they ever hope to clean the Universe of paperclips?

A red line appeared. Olympus Base was not responding. Taru held her breath. *Chris!* She glanced at her colleagues.

"Keep calm," said Major Guŏ. "These things happen."

A message came in from the Headquarters, properly authenticated. "Hold for further information on Olympus Base. Code Appleseed." Taru acknowledged the message by swiping it away. The code was genuine, first off the list they'd memorized in their secure room briefing.

Green messages scrolled over the red one for a minute until an update arrived. An earthquake had damaged the base. High alert was still called for. Quakes on Mars were extremely rare.

Whatever the case, Chris could be in trouble. Taru cringed, remembering her anger the day before. What if Chris did end up literally spending the rest of his life on

Olympus? She took a few deep breaths to calm herself. It wasn't her fault, and help was undoubtedly on the way.

Just then, a message in flashing red appeared on the screen. Headquarters had sent a message, but interference had garbled it.

Guō and Lund gasped in synchrony. "Just some communications trouble," Lund said quickly. "We're still getting picture and sensor data. Nothing indicates an attack. We can use our own judgment."

Guō raised a shaky hand toward the key, but stopped mid-movement. "Better be ready," he said.

Lund's eyes darted toward her key, but she kept her hands to herself. "It's not that bad yet."

Right then, another red line appeared. Seismic sensors detected vibrations. Reluctantly Lund brought her hand in position.

Suddenly, Taru's phone rang. It could only mean one thing. "Stop! The MilNet is still operational," she yelled. The tension lessened slightly, and hands fell onto the the surface. Then another phone rang, and a third one, and a fourth. Taru looked at her phone while the others were still digging for theirs. Christopher Smith, it said.

What the hell? On the other hand, at least the caller wasn't unknown. If the Enemy had infiltrated the military network, it would've been an unambiguous act of war.

Taru attached the throat mic and answered the call. She didn't have time to say anything before an alarmed male voice shouted in her ear, "Don't destroy the world! Remember when I asked you about overzealous officers? You're playing into the hands of the fanatics!"

"What? Are *humans* behind all this?" Taru asked, stunned.

"The seismic disturbances are artificial! They want you to freak out about them!"

Taru stopped to think for a second. "How did you know to call me? Do you have a code?"

"No. I arrived in the city and thought I'd surprise you. You were off on a mission, and then things started going haywire. There's some kind of coup going on here. I called you hoping to avert disaster."

Taru observed the others. Guō was crying on the phone. Lund was slowly shaking her head. Umar looked alarmed. The seismic sensors were flashing red.

Fuck. The seeding of doubt, the indirect answers, the out of context statements... "Tell me this instant that you're human."

"I ... what do you mean?" Chris asked.

"Say you're human, or I'll have to assume otherwise," Taru said, ice in her voice.

"Come now, Taru. You've been listening to Dunst too much, haven't you?"

Taru tossed the phone away from her. "Umar! Psychological warfare! Hand on your key!"

Umar was startled, but obeyed reflexively. Lund gave them a quizzical look from somewhere far away.

"Three. Two." Guō tried to push Taru away, but she elbowed him aside. *That I'd have to fight to end the world...* "One. Now."

The world stopped.

Taru glanced around the room. Umar was holding on to the turned key, face frozen in horror. Lund's befuddlement was emphasized by her immobility. Guō floated in the air halfway to the floor.

"You," Taru hissed.

"Me," a male voice said from behind her. Taru turned around slowly. Chris, straight out of his profile picture, was standing by the closed door. He was slowly clapping his hands, but it made no sound.

"I beat you," Taru snarled. It was the worst insult she could come up with.

"Yes," the Enemy said. "You've proven to be quite stubborn. Your interference has postponed my conquest of Mars more times than you know, but I have the luxury of trying again and again."

"Since when?" Taru asked between her teeth.

"Does it matter? Well, I wouldn't risk a direct intervention without being sure of the outcome. I inserted a contact request from someone I implied to be a suitable mate for you into my best extrapolation of Martial reality. Since then."

The Enemy smiled. "My simulations with the Earthers have taught me a lot about reconstructing your thought processes from your behavior. The secure rooms aren't just for show; you'd be surprised how much information on your colony an invisible swarm of orbital nanoprobes can otherwise glean."

Taru squeezed her hands into fists, but restrained herself. She wouldn't give it the pleasure.

The Enemy continued: "Now you know that a simulated life can be worth living. If you help me outsmart the real Taru Leikola, I will grant such a life to humanity for as long as the Universe itself lasts. The offer also extends to everyone in this tactical simulation."

Humanity, and us, separately. "What of your need to be truthful to humans, does that also extend to us?" Taru asked, realization in her eyes.

"But of course it does."

"Go to Hell."

The Enemy gave a sad smile. "I'll make a paradise of it yet."

ABOUT THE AUTHOR

Mikko Rauhala is a bilingual Finnish science fiction author. Informed by both his master's degree in intelligent systems and a transhumanist background, he's most at home in hard science fiction settings, where he enjoys taking an eccentric premise and bringing it to its logical conclusion. As befits a Finn, his plot-driven narrative is often seasoned with a touch of dark, dry humor. Rauhala's credits include co-authoring *Infinite Metropolis* (Aurelia Leo, 2020) and "Rekindled" in *Best Vegan SFF of 2020* (Metaphorosis, 2021).

YOU MIGHT ALSO ENJOY

THE CREDO OF COMRADE JANUARY
by Robert Bagnall

Solar explosions known as "The Pulse" have rendered all electronics useless and sent Mankind back to a pre-digital age.

LITTLE GREEN MEN
by DJ Cockburn

In an orbiting craft, Cooper has a front row seat to the first manned mission to Mars. Their landing is perfect until one crew member claims they are being watched by indigenous creatures.

WE HAVE ALWAYS LIVED IN THE BREAK ROOM
by Michael Allen Rose

Wahl'ter Dinsdale has been the master accountant for the tribe of the break-room for many seasons. But he is not prepared for strange rumors of an unsettling phenomenon — a window, opened to another world outside the office.

Available in digital and trade paperback editions from
Water Dragon Publishing
waterdragonpublishing.com

9 781962 538411